AF350143

Danny Right

DANNY RIGHT

This is a work of fiction. I made up almost everything. Well, I do know some folks who were in the Coast Guard. I've sat at the marina and watched offshore ships come and go. I've dreamed about the seas and what might go on...I stayed at a Holiday Inn Express last night.

Once again, I have to thank Deb for making this readable. I can't write a line without a boo-boo. If she doesn't like it, she let's me know. I should probably listen closer.

This book was made and printed in America and I'm big on that. To sell it without a cover is a no-no.

Cover design by Deb Gabel and Tommy Adkins. Published by Amazon and Asoda.

March 2022
ISBN: 9798429827285

This book dedicated to dreamers.

It's been one heck of a year. Stay strong. Love you guys.

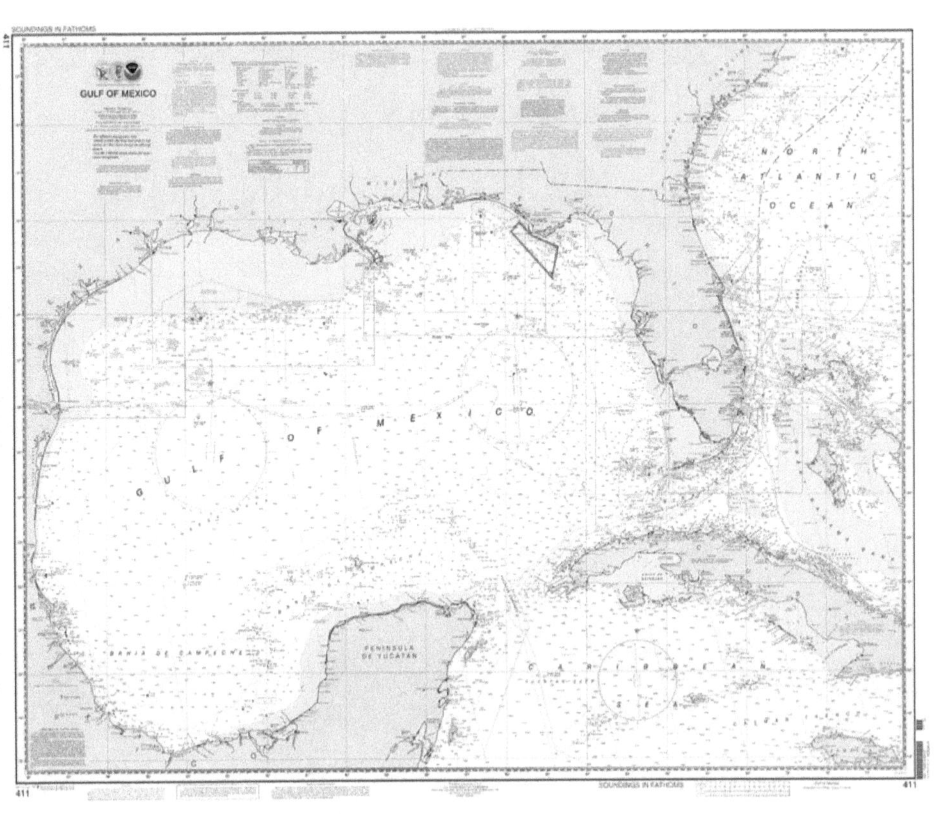

GULF OF MEXICO

Other Books by Tommy Adkins

Taters, Maters with Rice and Beans

Spinning Words

Blue Plate Special

Golden Isle
Join Our Golden Isle Facebook Page

Jim and Rose

The Katy Ann

Three Quarters Past a Lifetime

Sara's Italian Haunt

Apple Bay

Lloyd and the Wolf

Jeremiah Stone

Southern Folk Tales for the Holidays

DANNY
RIGHT

1

"**Y**ou must be Captain Right."
The large man on the bridge swiveled his plush chair around to face the stranger.
"No, no. Captain Right hasn't been with us in several years now. I'm Captain James."
"Well, actually, I meant his son, Danny."
"I understand. Danny never made captain. He didn't much care for captain duties. To tell the truth, he wasn't much cut out for captain. But he does love this ship. You must be the new engineer."
"Yes, sir. Donald Rig. Sorry I got things confused."

Captain James flipped a match and took a couple of puffs on his pipe, a half-bent Dublin that you would most always find him holding and all along even smoking.
"Danny will be working close with you. He keeps the engine room clean. Spotless,

I might add. Danny is what you might call
a little slow. Takes him time to think things
out. But he's a good man. Just in his
forties, I'd say. He came on this ship when
he was fourteen when his mom died with a
bad heart. He's been here ever since... even
after his dad passed years ago. I would
appreciated you treating him with respect."
"I try and treat everyone that way, sir. But I
understand. I certainly will."
"Down the stairs and down the hall you'll
find Rudy, your second, in the mess having
coffee. He will show you to your cabin.
It's right next to mine and just across from
the bunk house. Three days before we
make way so you can get acquainted with
the engines and equipment. Any questions,
get with Rudy. Need anything, get with
me."
"Thank you, sir. I'll just get my duffel. It's
out on the deck."
"Oh, Mr. Rig, welcome to the Just Right!"
"I look forward to it, sir."

Rig headed out onto the deck. He was a
large man, six foot two and around thirty.
More than capable of turning cranks and
moving large parts around an engine room.
He leaned over to pick up his duffel bag
when he noticed a fellow of middle size
dressed in a way too big t-shirt, baggy
jeans and high top Keds. The fellow leaned
over the railing looking out into the bay as
though he was searching for something. A
shaggy man, long hair, big beard, big belly
came bounding up the ramp onto the boat.
He yelled out, "Don't fall in, Danny!" The
man looking over the rail did not respond.

The man took a few steps on the deck and
held his hand out to Rig.
"I'm Gabby, First Mate. I'm the guy who
sits on the bridge and turns all the knobs
and flips all the switches."
Rig smiled and shook Gabby's hand.
"I'm Rig, the guy who hangs out in the
engine room and checks the oil."
Gabby gave out a Santa Claus laugh and

headed on inside the ship.

The sun had finally settled over the condos in the west. The lights were up on the ship. Little blue lights surrounding the ship's railing. White lights underneath lit up below the water line. Saint Andrews Marina was dimly lit, the waters of the bay now black. As Rig picked up his duffel, he turned to go inside but noticed Danny was now standing straight with his arm raised as though he was waving to something out in the bay. Rig looked in that direction but as far as he could see...nothing.

2

The big orange Panama City sun eased its
way down behind Bay Point across the bay
from the Just Right. Inside her hull in the
mess, Captain James, Donald Rig, Rudy
and Gabby sat around the table with coffee,
bringing Rig up to date on the everyday of
the Just Right.
"One thing for sure, if Danny ever walks by
and says there is a noise somewhere, you
need to pay attention. I don't know how he
does it, but he will hear a problem in the
engines. Heck, *anywhere* in the ship. If
there is a knock, a ping, any unusual sound,
he will pick it up right off," the captain
said.

He took a sip of his coffee and made a face
as he usually does when he tastes the ship's
coffee. Rudy took a sip of his and smiled.
He loved the ship's coffee.

"Beats anything I ever seen. He'll pick up
a partially blocked fuel line just from the
pitch of the engine."
Rig said "pretty impressive" as he looked
around the spacious mess, getting himself
comfortable with the new ship. He thought
to himself: *Sure... like he can __do__ that.*

A short - and real close to being fat - fellow
came through a swinging door. Braves cap,
ponytail hanging out the back. Two days
worth of black beard. Long apron covering
his t-shirt, baggy shorts. Skinny legs,
Crocs with white socks. Red sauce
splashed on the apron. Two inches of unlit
cigar out the side of his mouth.
"You fellows about ready for the evening
meal?"
He leaned over the table with his hand
extended to Rig.
"Pots. Virgil Pots, the Ship's Cook."
Rig took his hand.
"It's a pleasure."
"More like the ship's *chef.* Once you have

had one of his meals, you will beg to work this ship," the captain said as he grimaced through another sip of coffee.

"Of course, his coffee will make you want to hit the road running."

Everyone laughed but Pots.

Pots reached behind him and pulled a bottle of wine from the shelf.

"We don't sail tomorrow so we will have wine with the meal tonight."

He pulled a corkscrew from his apron pocket and began to uncork a bottle of Josh Cabernet.

"I was unable to hitch a ride over to Wine World at Watercolors today so a few bottles of Walmart will have to do."

Rudy got up and passed out glasses to everyone.

"Sounds good to me," he said as he sat back down.

"We gonna start with a little bruschetta, a little salad, the main course gonna be

Pasta Con Pomodoro e Basilico. I'm
toppin' it all off with an apple pie that
would make your grandma mad!"
He turned and walked back through the
swinging door.

Rig finished what may have been the best
meal he had ever experienced, excused
himself and retired to his cabin. He
thought for a few minutes about tomorrow
when he would go through the engine room
from top to bottom. Then he fell sound
asleep.

Danny stood at the railing just down from
the ship and waved at a disturbance out in
the black waters of the bay.

3

The next morning found Rig on the deck sipping steaming black coffee after a hearty breakfast of oatmeal, pancakes, maple syrup and spicy country sausage. The sun was just pushing itself over downtown Panama City. A dim light cast over the bay through a mist of rain and clouds from the west. Time for inspecting that engine room.

Rig flicked the last swallow of coffee over the side of the ship and just inside the cabin door was met by Gabby.
"Captain says you need to speed up your inspection and make ready to cast off in a couple hours. Something about helping the Coast Guard out with a stranded boat they are not able to get to due to a smuggler situation."

Rig stood there as though slapped in the face. Two hours was not enough time to check an engine room out that he had never seen. Gabby went back to the control console, Rig headed down the stairs. In the hall leading to the engine room, the Captain stepped from his quarters. Approaching Rig, he said:
"Try and get the engines up and warm in an hour. We need to get underway."
Rig turned to face him.
"An hour? I've never even been in the engine room yet. I don't know if that's possible, Captain."
The Captain stopped mid-stride.
"Rig, you a Democrat or a Republican?"
Rig had to stop and think for a second... confused by the question.
"A Democrat, sir."
"Well, you're the only one on board. But it don't matter in the least. I don't allow politics on the ship."
"Then why would you even ask that question?"

"Checking the size of your nuts."
The captain walked to the stairs to the
bridge. He stopped on the first step.
"Oh Rig?" Rig turned back toward him.
With his back to Rig, the captain said,
"I never accept opinion as fact."
He took the steps on into the bridge.

Rig followed the hall to the engine room,
still confused by the conversation. He
opened the engine room door and stopped
cold. The engine room gleamed like an
operating room. The two massive Cat
3508Bs shined like new. The floor was so
polished, you could eat off it. Danny stood
at the back of the room polishing a pressure
gauge. Without stopping, he said:
"They are warm, ready."

Rig walked to the back wall where the two
bright yellow buttons labeled ONE and
TWO were mounted. Rig pressed ONE
and the big diesel rattled but then ran as
smooth as any diesel could. The same with

TWO. The engine room filled with the noise of life and power. Rig cut the auxiliary generator and the ship took on a life of its own.

Rig looked over at Danny, shook his head and then pressed the intercom button.
"Captain, ready when you are."
Danny went back to polishing the pressure gauge.
"They sound good. They sound just right!"

4

Rig left the engine room with Danny and Rudy, satisfied that an engine room could not be in better shape. He grabbed a cup of coffee and made his way to the deck. The Just Right was easing its way through the pass. Rig watched the folks over at Saint Andrews State Park as the ship sliced its way into the waves of the Gulf.

Danny joined Rig with the Gulf air and salt spray in both their faces. Without making eye contact he said,
"Capt'n says meeting in the mess in thirty minutes."
He then looked over the railing, scanned the waters and walked back into the ship. Rig finished his coffee and went below.

The six men sat around the main table in the mess, even Danny. The Kongsberg auto pilot took the ship out into the Gulf.

Captain James took a sip of his coffee and made a face of distaste. Virgil Pots turned away acting as though he was hurt, but truth was he wasn't. Looking around at the men the Captain said,
"You men see we are short our normal crew. Coast Guard says we have to make room. We are headed down below The Keys to help a desperate boat of Cubans on a makeshift raft. We were first told a few folks on a raft. Now we are told there may be over two hundred. Two hundred clinging to a makeshift raft and of course there is a storm headed their way. We are starting to see a taste of it now. In another hour, we will be fighting the waves."

Pots got up to pour coffee for everyone.
"When you think we will reach these folks, Captain?"
"Tomorrow about sundown calculating from their coordinates. How will our

supplies hold up?”
“We should be fine although I’m not sure
for 200 folks. Guess I better get started
building sandwiches.”
“Gabby, what about fuel?”
“Fuel should be okay. It’s topped off.
Water could be a problem.”
The captain thought for a second.
“How is the de-sal?”
“Working full speed, but it won’t make
much difference in a day.”
“Very well. We will have to make do.
Everyone get as much rest as you can. The
next few days will be rough. Braves game
in the galley tonight!”
The captain got up and left the galley.
Everyone parted. Danny quipped “sounds
‘Just Right’” winked and went up to the
deck.

The overcast became thicker. The wind a
little stronger and the rain whipped
sideways from the west. Danny scanned
the waters from bow to stern. Then he saw

something roll in the water. A fin flipped as it dove. When it returned to the surface, he saw bright red hair. It was a woman. She waved! Danny waved back, not a bit surprised. Then she was gone...just like the last time.

The rain picked up. Danny stood there for a few moments and then pulled his hoodie over his head. Hands in his pockets, he continued to look out over the Gulf. He thought, *the captain was right. We'll be fighting the waves soon.* He turned and went below mumbling, "Sounds just right."

Rudy was on call and sat in the engine room for a while reading. Rig went to bed early. The captain took the first shift on the bridge, then Gabby would come on until morning. When Gabby came in around eleven, the captain went to bed and the Just Right went quiet. She plunged ahead in the darkness headed for the Caribbean.

5

Rafael was having second thoughts about putting his pregnant wife and six year old daughter on such a flimsy raft with so many people to escape his home land. His wife and daughter were dry on the makeshift boat, but he was clinging to the side. The rain, wind and waves were getting worse by the minute. Cries echoed over the dark rolling sea. He prayed for God's help.

~~~~~~~~~

Gabby picked up the sheet of paper in the fax tray. He read it and looked up at the captain who was just coming on the bridge. Outside, daylight was trying its best to be known. The captain took the fax from Gabby.
"Just what we need. A possible hurricane forming behind this storm."
Gabby got up from his chair.
~~~~~~~~~

"I'll be in my bunk until you're ready for all hands on deck."

He left the bridge. Captain James sat in the swivel chair and sipped his coffee as the rain bashed the windshield. He decided that when Rig was up and on duty he would ask for more speed. People were counting on him and he hated letting folks down.

~~~~~~~~

Rafael told his wife to wrap their daughter up in the old yellow raincoat he had found on the way to the boat. Suddenly, he heard screams as one of the brave husbands had let go of the raft and was dragged away by the waves. Rafael prayed. There had to be someone on the way to help.

~~~~~~~~

Captain James sat his coffee down on the top of the instrument panel. He couldn't wait any longer. The waves outside were growing and the rain was slamming the windshield harder. He hit the alarm button to signal 'all hands on deck!'

6

The National Weather Service in Tallahassee upgraded the storm to a hurricane, a Category One and named it Cindy. The Coast Guard sent a fax to the Just Right warning them and telling them they were no longer responsible for the folks in distress; it was too dangerous a request for a civilian boat.
The Just Right never received the fax.

About the time Gabby fell asleep the alarm went off. He rubbed his eyes, jumped from his bunk and made his way to the bridge... Rig, Rudy and Danny to the engine room... Pots to the galley… all waiting to see what was happening. The captain turned to Gabby as he entered the bridge.
"Gabby, when you get good and awake, I need you to check the deck. Make sure everything is secure. Take Danny with you."

He pressed the intercom and told Danny to
report to the bridge.

Rafael pulled with all his might and lifted
himself onto the boat in the space below his
wife's feet. Just enough room for him
although his legs hung over the side. The
wind grew stronger as Cindy gained
strength. The old makeshift boat tried its
best to stay together. Rafael took his wife's
hand straining to tell her everything would
be alright.

All outside lights went up on the Just Right.
The powerful spotlight on the bow tried its
best to drill through the waves and rain.
Danny ran to the bridge and he and Gabby,
rainsuits on, made their way to the deck.

7

Captain James sat in the swivel chair on the bridge. Lighting his pipe he briefly reflected on his years in the Coast Guard. Twenty two years. A hand full of medals and many missions to his name. He remained good friends with high ranking officers who he had promised always to be available if needed. The powers-that-be trusted James more than most of their current captains.

The radio on the dash gave a beep. He picked up the mike.
"The Just Right. James here."
"Philip, is that you?"
"Yes, go ahead."
"Commander Pitts here."
"Paul, I'll be damned. What brings you to a radio on a night like this?"

"Hell, Philip. I haven't been home yet.
Did you get our fax?"
"No sir... can't say we did."
"It was a notice relieving you from our
request to help this failing escape attempt."
"I can appreciate that, Paul, but we are way
too far into this to turn back now. We are
going to go ahead and do what we can."

Commander Pitts hung up the radio hand
set and picked up the land line. One ring
and it was answered. Pitts didn't wait for
an answer.
"Gary, I want you to make ready the
helicopter. Make it light, the weather is
going to be rough. Alert your best men.
I'll keep you posted."
He hung up. Now the call he dreaded, his
wife, to tell her it was going to be an all-
nighter for him. First he would make
coffee. Maybe a splash of brandy wouldn't
hurt.

On the deck Rudy and Danny faced rain
that was no longer falling down but
blowing sideways.
"Danny, you take the center. I'll check the
railing."
They both pushed their way into the wind
making sure the deck was secure. Rudy
grabbed a line whipping in the wind and
wrapped it. He then noticed Danny leaning
over the far rail waving at something in the
Gulf.

8

Rig stepped down into the engine room. He checked the oil pressure gauges and the pressure across the fuel filter lines. Temperature was good. He sat in the chair by the intercom. Leaned back against the wall. He closed his eyes for a second. He hadn't slept a wink the night before. His thoughts went to the past.

"Donnie, you take care of your ma now. I will be a little late tonight. We are re-working the engines on the old tug down by the docks."

A little late was right. A moment later, he was broadsided by an eighteen wheeler as he pulled out of the driveway. The driver had fallen asleep at the wheel and just plowed into his dad in their old Chevy Malibu. His dad was killed instantly.

For most of his days, Rig had taken care of his mom, his little sister and his aunt who lived with them. He got work at the local Caterpillar dealership and became the man on diesel engines. Then his mom passed, his aunt passed and his sister went to college. He became the engineer on the Miss Perl tug and there he stayed for almost ten years. Now the Just Right. Maybe he had found a home.

Cindy was not satisfied being a Category One. She huffed and puffed and became a Category Two. One hundred and four mile an hour winds barreled down on the make shift raft. Two hundred and twenty-three souls hung on for dear life. The tied-together raft slapped up and down on the warm Caribbean waters as Cindy was heading straight for them.

The Just Right topped a wave and fell sharply into a valley of Gulf water. Rig became weightless for half a second, but he

was wide awake as the Captain barked,
"Rig for bad seas!!" over the intercom.

Rudy and Danny fought their way back on
to the bridge. Shaking and pulling their
raingear off, Rudy asked,
"Captain, are you sure this is a good idea?"
"Rudy, this old tub can take it. That piece
of crap boat those folks are on ain't got a
prayer."
Rudy hung his raincoat on the rack by the
door.
"I'll be in the engine room with Rig."
Danny stood by the door dripping.
"Sounds just right."
"Danny, you get back to the engine room
and keep those ears open."
The captain turned to Gabby.
"Steady as she goes. It's going to get
rough."
Gabby thought, *GOING to?*

9

Pots looked around the galley thinking, *how can I possibly feed 200 people?* He opened up the cabinets and found a gallon jar of peanut butter. He knew there was all kinds of jelly in the cooler. Plenty of bread. He rested his hands on the counter for a moment and remembered when his dad had invited the whole First Federal little league baseball team over for snacks after practice. He remembered his dad said on the way home, "what the heck was I thinking?" His mom passed when he was ten. She told him "you always believed in your dad. He will take care of you, and Virgil, you behave." Pots remembered his dad made peanut butter and jelly sandwiches for the team and they enjoyed those sandwiches more than any prime rib, more than any pizza. His dad was the best. He made every one of those kids feel special. He knew his mom was right.

Pots pulled out the gallon of peanut butter,
the bread and jelly. He made them with
maybe just a little tear in one eye. He
wrapped them in cellophane. The ship
rocked and bounced off the waves and
some of the peanut butter got on his hands.
Pots, thinking of his dad, hoping he could
be half the man.

He also prayed that the Just Right would
get to the folks on the raft in time.
The intercom buzzed, "Pots."
"Captain, I got this."
"I knew you would."
The Just Right plowed into the storm.

Rafael and his family along with two
hundred more hung on in the makeshift
boat.

10

Two weeks ago, Rafael was living a happy life in Cuba. Poor but getting by in the town of Manzanillo. Then the new taxes were handed down and there was no way he could still feed his family. A paper was quietly passed around town to sign if you wanted to escape the grasp of the Cuban government. Rafael signed and volunteered to help build a boat. When all was said and done, two hundred and twenty-three folks had signed up to go, not counting their children.

The boat was a combination of jon boats, rubber rafts and wooden rigging. A very old fifty horse Evinrude was strapped on the back. A few weeks passed and homes and animals were left behind. Crying could be heard all over the makeshift boat.

The first few days the weather were perfect.
Flat seas. The old Evinrude barely moved
the cluster, but they made headway and
Cuba was in the past.

Six days out the clouds rolled in, the wind
picked up and the old outboard conked out.
A flimsy sail pulled the raft on north.
Rafael along with eight other men slipped
over the side and hung on in order to keep
the raft above the waves. The waters were
warm and at first it wasn't so bad.

11

Rudy and Danny entered the engine room
still wiping water from their faces and hair.
"Number two is running a little slow.
Probably fuel filter," Danny announced as
soon as he got on into the room.
"Come on, Danny. I don't hear any
difference and we changed filters right
before we left."
Rudy continued brushing water away.
"You better listen to him, boss."

Rig checked the tachometers and sure
enough, the number two engine was about
three hundred RPMs slow. He looked back
at Danny.
"But we got new fuel back at the dock in
the number one tank."
"It's bad fuel," Danny said, shaking his
head. He walked over to the storage room

to get a new filter.

Rig slapped the intercom button.
"Captain, I'm going to shut number two
down for just a couple of minutes. Dirty
fuel filter on the way to stopping up."
"Bad timing, Rig. Make it fast. I'm kinda
partial to this old boat. Don't want to lose
her from a bad damn filter."
"Rudy, shut her down and be ready to
restart."

Danny brought up the new filter. Rig
closed the valves, spun the nuts and
dropped the filter housing. New filter in,
nuts tight and valves open.
"Okay, Rudy, bring her back on line."
She spun and growled and refused to crank
at first. On the third try she came to life.
Rig, Rudy and Danny all took deep breaths.
Over the intercom: "She's back on line,
Captain."
"Good job, Rig."

Taking a close look at the old filter, Rig
found that it was almost full of sand. He
looked at Danny.
"So. I won't be doubting you again."

Danny walked over with a rag and began
cleaning where the old filter had been
laying on the floor.
Rudy came over, took the old filter, put it in
the new box and dropped it into the trash.
"Anyone for coffee?"
Rig: "Sure."
Danny: "Orange juice."
Rig: "Make mine an orange juice too."
Rudy headed for the galley.

12

Rudy brought Rig and Danny their orange juice and then returned to the galley where Pots had peanut butter and jelly sandwiches stacked high. Danny and Rig sat in two folding chairs by the gauge panel. Rig took a sip of his juice.

"Say, Danny. I was just wondering who it was you were waving to back at the dock. Rudy mentioned you did the same on deck when you guys were out there making the tie downs."

Danny was slow to answer. He looked away from Rig.

"A friend."

"A friend out in the water."

"Yes, a friend..."

"I don't mean to dispute you, but a friend out in the water just don't seem likely."

"A friend, a lady friend. She waves at me."

Just then the Just Right was making its way
over a rogue wave. It fell ten, maybe
fifteen feet into the trough between waves.
Rig stumbled over to the intercom.
"Captain."
"Yes, Rig, we are okay but go ahead and
prepare for more of the same. We are
getting into heavy waters."
The intercom went silent. Rig looked out
over the engine room seeing Danny still
sitting in his chair sipping his juice
thinking, *I really wasn't expecting this.*

The night pushed its way to morning. The
daylight in the east made a feeble attempt at
making light. The Just Right plowed its
way ahead toward the folks hanging on to
the thrown-together raft. They should
make it before sundown if all goes well.

Pots made coffee, scrambled eggs, boiled
grits and fried bacon. No one could sleep
but everyone would eat.

13

Captain James stood at the center port hole on the starboard side of the ship. Outside was almost as dark as night. An eery light cast over the rolling waters. The Just Right was rising and falling at a steady pace now. He remembered back when he was a boy in Fairhope, Alabama. In the summer he would lay on his back after supper behind his folks' house and stare at the sky. The moon, the stars, the blackness that went on forever. *How could that be*, he would think. *How could all of this just happen?* Now, the endless rolling seas made him think the same. And just then as before, he knew there was a God. How else could all of this be? He closed his eyes and prayed for all the folks he was on his way to help.

Rafael was so exhausted, he had to do doze off. Suddenly a scream from his daughter

brought him fully awake. The waves were
slapping them all over the place. This tied-
together wreck they had made had to be on
the verge of coming apart.

Gabby called out.
"The worst is on us now, Captain. The eye
should be coming up soon. With a little
luck, we will be arriving at the rescue in the
eye!!"

Captain James ended his prayer by
thanking God.

Rafael rose to his knees to hold his
daughter and noticed the waves were
calming. Off to the east sunlight was doing
its best to poke through the clouds.
Everyone hanging on for dear life was
praying this nightmare was soon over with.

Rig was concerned with the fuel supply
after the bad gas they had put in in Tank
One. Rudy constantly checked the pressure
gauges knowing the diesels were straining.
Danny polished the valves, always
cleaning. Pots waited with sandwiches
ready. It was all he could do. Gabby sat
back in the swivel chair on the bridge,
confident the ship was strong enough for
this storm.

Captain James held onto the console and
watched, a cloud of doubt raced through his
mind. Ten minutes later, that doubt went
the way of the storm when the Just Right
broke through a wall of rain and the seas
were calm. The sun shined down on a lake
of emerald green.

14

Rudy swung his chair around to face the Captain.

"I got an idea."

Captain James pulls himself away from the porthole.

"Let's hear it, Rudy."

"We align the Just Right alongside the raft. Tie their rig onto our ship. I'll adjust the GPS, radar and auto pilot to align the ship with the storm and match its speed. We should be able to stay inside the eye until we have everyone on board."

"Good thinking, Rudy. It's a plan!"

Captain James hit the intercom button and explained the plan to Rig. Rig explained to the Captain his concern over the fuel problem.

"We should burn much less fuel while in the eye. Just keep me posted."

"Will do."

Rig cut the transmission to the bridge and shook his head at Rudy.

"It's going to be close."

Rafael was about to make the second worst mistake of his life besides putting his wife, child and himself on the ragged boat. He stood in front of his wife and called to the crowd hanging onto the raft.

"It's over! The worst has past and we can breath again. We will make it to shore now."

He sat back down and hugged his wife and daughter. Tears in all of their eyes.

The Just Right plowed through the water at full speed. Captain James spotted the raft full of people ahead with his binoculars.

"All ahead full, Rudy!"

Danny paused in his effort to make every valve shine.

"There is a rattle in number two."

Rig paused and listened but did not hear it. Somehow he knew it was there.

15

$\mathbf{A}$ rip-tearing sound, a loud clank and an abrupt stop. Smoke began to boil from engine two. Rudy ran for the fire extinguisher. Rig pushed Danny aside to check the rear of number two. Smoke coming from everywhere, hard to tell exactly where. Rig hit the intercom button.
"Captain, we have lost number two!
The Captain came back with sarcasm.
"Rig, I hope you're not saying that's bad news. Right now is not a good time."
"We will see what we can do."
Rig knew it was useless; probably a blocked injector. The engine tried to over-compensate for water in the fuel. A broken injector flew through the engine to no telling where, mass destruction on the way.
Rig back to the captain:
"Captain, you have one engine. You're going to have to deal."

Captain James slammed the intercom
closed.
"Gabby, we have only one engine!"
Gabby flipped the autopilot off and grabbed
the control stick.
The Just Right now cut thought the smooth
water like a warm knife through butter.

Rafael spotted the ship on the horizon. He
hugged his wife, smiled and told her they
were going to be okay. Kissed his daughter
on the forehead and wiped tears from her
eyes.

Captain James held the binoculars to his
eyes. He spotted the raft and the people
holding onto it.
"Gabby, I don't think we have enough
room..."

16

Captain James pulled the binoculars down and stared out at the vast waters. He turned to Gabby.

"First thing we are going to have to do is get rid of the crane."

Gabby kept his attention on their headway. "But Captain, that's a quarter million dollars' worth of nuts and bolts back there. Besides that, we just painted it."

"Doesn't matter. We are going to need every inch. Tell Rig and Danny to meet me on the stern."

Gabby pressed the intercom button and told Rig and Danny to meet the captain on the stern by the crane. Then he switched to the galley and told Pots to make the life rafts ready for launch. He guided the Just Right closer to the hoard of people hanging on for dear life.

Outside, the water was calm enough but the clouds were low and they boiled and rolled over, angry.

Rafael slipped back into the water to give his wife and daughter more room, only this time he found that he was too weak to hang on. Sinking underneath the water, he looked up to see his wife's arms reaching out for him. Too weak to swim to the surface, he could only watch.

Something from below grabbed his legs and lifted him back to the surface. His wife reached out for him and helped him to cling to the raft. She held onto him with all the strength she had. He turned to look but all he saw was a large tailfin diving back under the water. In the distance, he could see a ship but he could no longer hold his eyes open.

17

Captain James, Rig and Danny walked out on the deck headed toward the crane but they stopped and looked around them. The Just Right sat in calm waters surrounded by an almost perfect circle of black rolling clouds and rain. Surreal. Something right out of a syfi movie. This was something only bad dreams were made of, but at the same time, strangely beautiful. The captain stood for several seconds speechless, then said,
"We have to get this crane off the deck. Ideas..?"
Danny pulled his attention from the scene.
"We drive it over."
Rig looked at the captain.
"Simple enough."

The crane was a four wheel frame with a

small cockpit on the front for a driver. A
twenty foot arm that stretched out the back,
then extended to forty feet. A cable with a
hook hung from the arm.
Before anyone could say anything else,
Danny jumped into the cockpit, flipped the
key and pressed the start button. The
engine came to life, idling high for warm
up. Danny eased it in to gear and let off the
clutch. The crane lunged forward, Danny
leaped from the cockpit.

He hit the deck standing but as the crane
rolled off the stern, the hook on the end of
the crane caught Danny's arm. The crane
sank fast and pulled Danny with it. Captain
James pulled the radio from his back
pocket.
 "All stop!! Man overboard!!"
Gabby reacted immediately. He threw the
Just Right into reverse for a second, then
into neutral. Rig jumped into the dark
waters and dove down as fast as he could
but the crane and Danny were nowhere in
sight.

18

Rig held his arm up and Captain James pulled him back aboard the Just Right. Rig bent over, hands on knees catching his breath. He looked up at the captain and shook his head. Captain James took a few seconds and pressed the button on the radio.
"Gabby, get us over by the raft so we can start transferring people."
"Aye aye, Captain!"
Gabby eased the throttle forward and the ship edged its way toward the raft.

Danny could feel soft lips on his and warm air filling his lungs. He opened his eyes but was now moving through the water too fast to keep them open. Hand in hand with someone or something. All he saw was long flowing red hair. Danny reached up

and Rafael pulled him over the edge of the
raft. Danny blew water from his mouth,
shook his head and sat up. Looking for the
Just Right, he spotted it heading their way.
Danny looked past the Just Right to see the
storm's wall of anger approaching.
Rafael asked Danny, "Are you alright??"
"I'm not sure…."

Rig was back in the engine room with
Rudy, both concerned if the remaining
engine would last. Captain James thinking
how could Danny be gone?

On the raft, folks were clapping, whistling,
yelling with hopes they would be saved.
Captain James stood on the deck with a bull
horn.
"Everyone remain calm! We will bring you
aboard in an orderly fashion. It's going to
be rough but we will get you out of here."
Unfortunately very few understood
English.

Captain James thinking *only if this storm does not strengthen.*

From Tallahassee, NOAA had just upgraded the hurricane to a Cat 3.

19

Captain James was ecstatic to see Danny. Waving, he clicked the radio to Gabby and told him to relay the good news. Gabby pulled the Just Right alongside the raft. The first one to hit the deck was a Jack Russell-looking mutt, soaking wet, who ran to the cockpit and laid down next to the door. Next was Danny who met the arms of Captain James.
"So glad you're okay, son! You had us scared. Now let's get this raft tied onto the Just Right."

The two went about throwing lines to some of the guys on the raft securing the makeshift raft to the ship. The radio buzzed in the captain's pocket.
"Captain, we are going to have to move! The eye wall is closing in on us fast."

"You can go ahead and start easing toward
the center of the eye. We are close enough
to being secure and we are going to start
bringing these people on board."
Captain James turned to Danny.
"Do any of these folks speak English?"
"Rafael."
"Tell him to let them know to come on
aboard. But one at a time, calmly."

The ideal way would be for the old, then
the women and children to come on board
first but that would mean folks climbing
over each other and that was not an option.
So one at a time, in order of seating, they
made their way to the deck of the Just
Right.
"Gabby, I need Pots and Rigs on the deck
to help with placement of these people."
"Will do, Captain!"

Rigs hit the deck showing the old, women
and children below deck. Filling the galley
and all state rooms. Pots confronted the
Captain.

"Are you sure about this? These people are breaking the law of their own country. Asking for help in our country where they don't belong. We barely made it this far with two engines. What makes you think we can make it out of here overloaded with one? Captain, we are risking our lives and this ship for people who don't belong."

Gabby pushed the throttle forward and turned the wheel left to the center of the eye.
"Pots, you volunteered for this trip. You knew that there was a storm and the danger."
"Didn't volunteer for no hurricane, Captain. These people are risking all our lives."
"Listen Pots, you're welcome to get off the ship anytime you like. You can even take one of the life rafts. Now pardon me, I'm busy."
For the first time, Captain James heard Danny laugh.

Pot's relit the cigar stuffed in his mouth and
walked back into the cockpit.
Captain James knew Pots was a hothead
and at times a bit heartless but damn, he
was a good cook.

The last, an old woman, tried to make her
way up on the deck but kept slipping back.
She no longer had the strength. Danny, still
dripping wet, jumped back on the raft and
lifted her up. Danny jumped back on board
and helped the Captain cut the raft loose.
The Just Right was full. Down below and
on deck... not room for another soul.

20

Captain James pressed the button on the radio.

"By the way, Pots. We have a special guest on the deck beside the door. He will be needing some meat and fresh water, pronto!"

The Just Right slowly eased its way toward the center of the eye leaving the raft behind. The raft bounced its way closer to the wall and was finally consumed by the force of the hurricane. It was flipped up on end, turned around and then ripped apart before it disappeared from sight of the Just Right.

The captain's radio buzzed.
"Captain, we have two choices. Both to the south where the hurricane is most narrow.

Golden Isle or Jamaica, both about the
same distance."
"Make it Jamaica, Gabby. They have ships
that could help us out."
"Jamaica it is, Captain."
Gabby slowly turned the Just Right to the
southern wall of the eye.

"Danny, I'm going to need ropes run every
three feet on the deck. From cockpit to aft.
And stern to cockpit. These people have
got to have something to hang onto."

The Captain made his way back into the
cockpit. Danny, with the help of Rafael,
strung the ropes and explained to the
people how best to hold on.

First the rain, then the wind, then the waves
tossed the Just Right about like a ping pong
ball. The people on the deck hung on for
dear life.

Danny made his way to the cockpit door,

opened it and the dog ran inside. It took all
of his strength to close the door. The ship
bounced and was pounded by the waves.
The dog ran down the steps directly to the
galley where an old woman sat at the table
nursing a hot coffee. He made a whimper
and laid by her side.

21

The Aerial Reconnaissance Weather
Officer, Kyle Stokes, relayed to the pilot
that he had all the data he needed. Over
radio, Stokes told the clerk back in
Lakeland:
"This thing is now bouncing on at 150 mph
and growing, 920 millibars and falling. I
don't recall a storm gaining strength this
fast. The eye is almost a perfect circle."
The WC-130J Super Hercules veered off
the storm's path headed back to Lakeland.

Commander Jane Reels at the Coast Guard
station in Key West picked up the phone.
"Jane, this is Paul Pitts, Panama City,
Florida. I need your help if possible. I
have an offshore vehicle in the middle of
this storm trying to save some folks leaving
Cuba. It's starting to look like trouble."

"I have the Key Biscayne ready and
waiting to launch but it's looking awful
nasty out there. Not sure we can handle
that weather."
The Key Biscayne sat full crew and ready.
The water around Key West was already
getting choppy - telling everyone there was
something big out there.

Without turning his head from the job of
steering the ship, Gabby said,
"Captain, we are no longer receiving
communication from the shore."
This monster out in front of them had no
mercy.
"Captain?"
"Steady as she goes, Gabby. We will bust
out of this soon."
A blast of wind almost blew Captain James
down and then stopped. James turned
around and looked out the window in the
cockpit door. Of all people, it was Pots out
on deck seeing that folks were hanging on
to the ropes. The wind and waves took the

little fat man down several times but he
would grab a rope and hang on. Slipping
and sliding, he made his way across the
deck encouraging folks and helping them to
hang on.

Captain James pushed through the door and
was able to slam it closed. The wind
caught him and he slid down but was able
to grab hold of one of the ropes. He made
his way over to Pots, slipping and groping
from rope to rope.
"Pots, get your ass back inside the cockpit!
That's an order!"
Pots looked at him and kept on checking
the people hanging on for dear life.
Captain James helped trying his best to
comfort the folks on deck. Pots made his
way back to the door of the cockpit. James
was right behind him.
"Pots, you're a fool. But a good fool. Now
get in the galley and stay put."

The Just Right fell into its first valley of

water and powered its way up the other
side.

The lone engine stayed strong. Screams
were heard from the deck. The captain
tried the radio.
"Mayday, mayday!"

No reply.

22

Captain James looked out the front windows on the bridge. The windshield wiper made no dent in the pounding rain. The wind...well, he hoped the glass held. He let himself escape for a second. He thought how good it always feels when after an ordeal is over, how good it is to sit back, relax, knowing you're done with the bad that had gone on. A good meal, a long shower, a relaxing bed, a cool breeze blowing in through the open window by your bed. Sometimes the aftermath of something that had gone way bad was almost worth it. The feeling of *it's over*. He was shaken back to the present when the Just Right hit a wall of water.

Rig and Rudy were hovering over every gauge and valve in the engine room. They were doing their best to see to it that the

only engine left was holding its own. Rudy
was fighting back the only bout with sea
sickness he had ever known. He was
already realizing once would be enough.

In the galley Pots dumped a can of Vienna
Sausages into a bowl and mashed them up.
He took them out to the dog curled up by
the old lady. He scarfed the sausage up in
three bites. Spun around three times and
laid back down. He was snoring before
Pots could pick up the bowl.

Gabby, still keeping his eyes straight ahead
asked the captain:
 "Sir, what about all of those folks out on
the deck. How are they surviving? How
many are still there?"
"I don't know, Gabby. Probably not
many."
Captain James picked up the log. Two
hundred and forty-two souls had been
counted coming aboard.

Rafael hung on with all his might.
Knowing his wife and daughter were safe
inside gave him strength. The man next to
him was gone and the one just below him
was no longer there. At times, the wind
picked Rafael up and slammed him back to
the deck. The rain made it impossible to
see.

"Key West to Panama City. Cindy has been
upgraded to a Cat 5. The Key Biscayne
will be waiting on the south end near
Jamaica for the Just Right to break through.
We are not able to enter the storm for
rescue!!"
Commander Paul Pitts replied with
"I understand."

23

Captain Mike stood on the bridge of the Key Biscayne looking through the window at the back side of this monster storm they named Cindy. A slight smile came over his face because his ex-wife's name is Cindy. The slight smile turned into a grin thinking how well it fits. His grin and smile turned into a frown as his thoughts turned to the Just Right, knowing it was in the thick of this mess with way too many folks on board. He pondered for the fourth time about going in. Head strong. His whole life he had fixed things. Now he felt his hands were tied. Risking the lives of his crew was out of the question. He turned his thoughts to his daughter. His daughter was turning into her mother. Not good. Just not good. Three Hurricane Cindys were too many.

He turned to his first.
"Steady as she goes."
Captain Mike did a double take.
"Who the hell are you?!!"
"Just coming on my shift, sir. I'm your new helmsman, Ensign Jamal Smith from Pensacola."
"I don't need your history. Do you know how to drive this thing??"
"Yes, sir. Best in my class."
"Best in your class, really…. How 'bout experience??"
"My first assignment, sir."
The captain looked out at the raging seas ahead of them.
"That's great, son. Just great."

Captain Mike Fran was due to retire in six months with 22 years under his belt with The Coast Guard.
"Tell me, ensign, you ever been on the bridge of one of these things?"
"Oh yes, sir. In order to graduate, we had

to go through several complicated
maneuvers. I passed with flying colors.”
The captain moved around closer to the
windows, thinking a beer sure would be
good about now.

The Just Right was pushed back,
completely out of the water for a second.
The engine screamed with no resistance.
Danny looked over at Rig.
“Not good, boss! Not good!”

The children cried, the young women
called for help, the old women hung their
heads and prayed.

24

The old man clicked 'save' as Chapter 24 of his new book was finished. He got up from his desk and walked to the sliding glass doors. Out on the balcony of his 15th floor condo, he looked out over The Gulf. In the distance he could see the first signs of Cindy. A wall of black. The wind had picked up and the waves were beating the shoreline below. He closed the door, walked around and poked his head out the bedroom door.

"What did Ross say about the storm?"
His roommate called back.
"He said it was the fastest moving hurricane he had ever seen."
She paused a second.
"Said it was too late to leave now. Even though it's a Cat 5, the roads are gridlocked. 231 is a parking lot. We'll be okay, won't we?"

"Of course. This is a strong building. 15
floors up, no problem with flooding. It will
come and go before we know it. I'll be
pouring wine in the kitchen shortly."

He closed the door and thought,
*I sure hope the young man they had met at
Harry's Bar a few nights ago, the one that
told them about the mermaid, wasn't out in
that storm.*

~~~~~~~~

Danny looked over at Rig and shook his
head again. He said, "Not good."
He made his way out of the engine room
stepping over people mashed together in
the hall leading to the bridge. The Just
Right fell into a valley of water. Danny
landed on the people lining the floor.
The rain was too hard now to see anything.
~~~~~~~~

Captain Mike spun around to face Ensign Jamal.

"Ensign, you got something to say?"

"Yes, sir, I d….."

"First of all, Ensign, I need you to make a line back and forth, about a mile. I don't want to miss anything coming out of the back side of this storm."

"Yes, sir, got it."

"Go ahead and tell me what's on your mind."

25

"**Y**ou know, Captain, if those poor folks on that boat out there do make it through this storm, if they do make it to the states and apply for citizenship and go through the channels the right way, they still ain't got a chance."
"I don't guess I understand what the hell you're talking about, Smith."
"Well, probably why I won't ever make captain, sir."
"For goodness sake, Smith, what's wrong with you?"
"Minority, sir. Don't know if you noticed, sir, but I'm black."
The captain walked closer to the window of the bridge.
"To tell ya the truth, Smith, no... I hadn't noticed. I don't think being black, brown, yellow or green makes you stupid. I just think it makes you a minority in the US."

"You ever been to Jamaica?"
"No, sir."
"White folks are the minority there. Less successful white folks than black. Mexico, less successful white folks than brown. China, less successful white folks than whatever damn color they are. It ain't about the color you are, it just works out in the math."

Smith didn't say anything. The captain stared straight ahead.
"Besides that, Smith, those people out there on that boat, no matter what color, they are children of God. Just like we all are. In His eyes, very successful and that's most important. The most successful any of us can be is trying our best in the eyes of God. Taking care of each other."

Smith stared ahead. Captain Mike stared ahead too.
Smith said, "Alright then, Captain. Let's go ahead and go into this monster!"

26

"Hit the alarm, Smith. Rig for rough seas.
All ahead full!"
"Yes, sir!"
The Key Biscayne leaped forward. The
waves grew higher, the wind and rain much
stronger.
"It's just a hunch, Smith, but head west
north west."
The 110 foot cutter plowed through much
rougher seas than it was meant for.

Danny tripped, fell and stumbled back onto
the bridge. Captain James held onto the
console.
"Danny, you don't have to but I need
someone to load the escape pod with as
many people as can be stuffed into it.
Maybe if we are lucky - 20."
Gabby was doing his best to keep the Just
Right afloat.

"Captain, you really think there are 20 left out there?"
Danny didn't say anything as he pushed his way through the door out onto the deck.

The rain came in sideways now, so strong it hurt when it hit your face. Danny could barely see. He made his way to where Rafael had been hanging onto the rope. He wasn't there. No one was there; the back deck was empty. Danny struggled and clawed his way back to the bridge door. He looked up and could barely make out someone climbing the ladder to the top of the bridge where the escape pod was mounted. Rafael was holding the door open as the men entered. The last man in, Rafael climbed inside and closed the door.

Another monster wave hit the Just Right, the wind blew and Danny was gone….
washed away to the stern. He had one chance to grab the railing. He did for a second but could not hold on. He was gone.

27

Rafael showed the fellow sitting in the top seat of the lifeboat how to release the boat and how to crank the little engine once the boat became upright. It was a quick lesson of how to run and launch the boat. Then Rafael, head down against the wind, backed out of the boat into the raging weather. He could not leave his wife and child. He opened the door to the bridge and stumbled in. Stepping over the three women sitting on the floor, he made his way to his wife who was holding his daughter in the captain's chair. His wife cried out in tears thinking that Rafael had drowned.

Gabby did not move his eyes from the windshield but said,
"Captain, we have no room."
Captain James turned his head to Rafael holding his wife and child.
"Deal with it!"

Then he turned his head back to the job at
hand.

Pots dug through the cabinets and came up
with five life jackets. There would be more
on the bridge and in the engine room. Rig
and the captain would pass them out. Since
he had only five, he handed them to the
oldest packed into the galley. The old lady
with the dog shook her head no and turned
the jacket down. Pots knelt down with
intentions of wrapping the life jacket
around the dog. He thought better of it and
patted the dog on the head. The old woman
smiled, Pots handed the jacket to one of the
younger women.

Pots remembered for a second all the dogs
in his life. One in particular. One that
stuck by him through thick and thin, and
there was an awful lot of 'thin'. Pots
thought and wondered just how many cans
of dogfood he had opened. He remembered

exactly how Alpo Chop House in Gravy
smelled. She always said 'Get Alpo, it's
the best'. It smelled good and he kinda
wished he had a can to open for this dog
right now.

The Just Right fell into a gully and almost
turned sideways. Everyone aboard was
lifted off the floor for half a second. For
the first time ,Captain James was not sure
they would make it out of this storm.

28

The remaining engine stalled when the
Just Right hit bottom in the valley of water.
Rig held his breath but was able to breathe
when the engine took off running again.
He stood for a second resting on the
pressure gauge.

He remembered when his dad had bet their
next-door neighbor twenty dollars that his
lawn mower would crank on the first pull
after sitting all winter without running. Mr.
Higgins laughed out loud and put his beer
down on the table by the storage shed in the
backyard. He pulled twenty dollars from
his wallet and threw it on the table.
"You're on!"
Rig's dad pulled the mower out of the shed
and let it set in the sun for a few minutes.
He checked the gas and pumped the little
black ball to fill the carburetor with gas.

His dad caught his son's eye and winked.
He looked over at Mr. Higgins with a
smirk. Then he pulled the mess out of the
cord on top of the mower. The old mower
coughed and sputtered. Rig held his breath
then too. A puff of black smoke rolled
from the mower and lo and behold, it
rattled to life. Rig's dad picked up the
twenty. Mr. Higgins picked up his beer
took a swallow. "I'll be damn….."

The Just Right rolled to its portside and Rig
lost his footing. Slipping down, he hit his
head on the edge of the engine mount. He
was out cold laying on the floor. Ruddy
hung to the sink in the washroom thinking
being this sick, how could he live? He
looked up into the mirror and remembered
his first year in little league baseball.

He played first base for First Federal Bank.
He smiled for a second forgetting his
sickness. He could catch any ball ever
thrown to him - bar none, but could not bat

for crap. The Strikeout King.

He dropped his smile. He could hear the
engine straining. Where the hell was
Danny?

29

$\mathbf{D}$anny flew through the water as fast as before. Hand in hand with someone. So fast he couldn't open his eyes. Jumping from wave to wave with just enough time to take a breath.

Ensign Smith did his best as an inexperienced helmsman to keep the ship straight but for him it was a losing battle. Captain Mike stepped up.
"I'll take it from here, son." And he took control.
"This storm is much more than I bargained for. We are going to have to turn back."

Smith stumbled up to the window, feeling hurt and embarrassed. He followed the spotlight scanning the rolling waves.
"Captain, there is something or someone out there. A bright red flashed in the spot

that we just rolled by. I couldn't tell but it damn sure looked like a woman!"

"You better be right, Smith. If I risk my ship on a hallucination of yours, I'll chew your ass."

Captain Mike hit the intercom.

"All stop! Bring that spot back around to the bow. Get some men and a net starboard!"

Four men with foul weather gear strapped themselves to the railing. They threw the net over the side. The spotlight reflected on a flash of red again. Two of the four men could tell it was hair.

It was a woman.

Danny was picked up and out of the water and into the net. He grabbed ahold of it and the four men pulled him aboard.

Falling over onto the deck, Danny passed out. One of the four men watched the red hair disappear below the raging waves.

The Key Biscayne turned and was full speed ahead out of the storm.

30

Gabby could barely see anything in front
of them now. Captain James still trusted
him to control the ship, but then he realized
what he was doing had little effect on what
the Just Right responded to. The waves
were taking them where ever they liked.
The wind made some corrections all along.

Gabby looked again and thought he could
see something. He rubbed his eyes. He
could see the kitchen in the house he grew
up in. He could see the light pine paneling.
He could see the yellow phone hanging on
the wall with the dial on the front. He
smiled at the extra long cord on the hand
set that he finally talked his dad into
getting. He could remember the number
after all these years and the Randalls next
door on the party line. He could remember

his mom calling out for him to go to bed after he had talked to Karen way too long after supper.

The Just Right slammed into another wall of water and fell into a deep trough. Gabby could no longer see anything, but he could feel the ship tilting way too far.

Captain James stumbled and tripped but was able to hold onto the console. He reached into his pocket for his lighter and for the first time in two days, he lit his pipe. At the first puff, the windshield blew in and the bridge was flooded with water. Before Captain James hit his head on the console, he heard the crash of the Just Right slamming into the escape pod.

31

Rafael's wife was holding their daughter who was sound asleep. She imagined a green tricycle barreling down the hall. Full speed, her little girl meant business and would make it to the living room in record time....
The water pouring in through the broken windshield brought her back to the grim reality of the moment.

As the spotlight scanned the waters behind them, Captain Mike got a glimpse of a ship. A ship flipping over in mid-air.

The Just Right flipped in the Gulf just like a toy boat in a Jacuzzi. Over and over, then high into the air. It sank on impact. The angry beast of this storm swallowed it.

The Coast Guard helicopter from Miami radioed Panama City.

"Commander Paul Pitts. I'm afraid the ship
you asked about is gone."
Commander Pitts laid the radio phone
down and turned around in his chair. He
should get home now. His wife would be
worried. The wind outside was getting
stronger. Soon the storm would be here.

He pulled a cigar from his desk drawer.
A Cuban. He lit it and poured a shot of
Single Barrel Jack. He would make it
home soon enough and sleep with his wife
all safe and sound in their beach home. For
now, for the next few minutes, he had to
talk with God.

32

Captain Mike paused for a second and then made a beeline to the intercom.
"All stop! Is that fellow we brought on board awake?"
The voice on the other end:
"He's just now coming around, Captain."
"I'm on my way. Smith, turn this boat around and stay put. Keep your eye trained on those waters."
"Yes, sir!"
Smith was confused but followed orders as he was told.

Captain Mike pulled a chair up to the bunk where Danny lay.
"What's your name, son?"
Danny trying his best to focus. "Danny."
"Son, I need you to give me the layout of

the Just Right. Do you know it?"
"I know the Just Right."
"Danny, are the doors from the bridge, galley and engine room water tight?"
"Just Right, all doors are just right."
Captain Mike turned to his side.
"Tell Smith to ease back into the storm. As close to where that ship went down as he can."
"Yes sir, Captain."

The message was relayed and the Key Biscayne made its way forward. The waters were mad but not near as bad as before.

33

When the glass broke and the captain went tumbling on the floor over the top of several other folks, Gabby stumbled his way across the room. He grabbed Rafael's wife and daughter, then pushed them through the door leading down the hall and slammed it behind them turning the latch. Pots clawed his way over a mountain of people who were thrown all over the galley. He pushed the door closed and made it secure. Ruddy pulled a few people into the engine room relieving the crowded hallway. He closed the door and made it tight.

The Just Right was sinking fast. No one on the bridge, the deck or the escape pod survived. Pots knew the watertight doors would hold for a while, but the oxygen would run out shortly and who knows how deep the Gulf was here.

The storm finally blew on passed and the waters around The Key Biscayne grew calmer. Smith kept her in place as ordered as he watched for the ship. Back on the bridge, Captain Mike called out over the intercom again.
"I need a couple of volunteers for deep water diving!"

Before he could turn around, there was a callback from the communication room. "Captain, you have five volunteers, sir. The twins and three new guys!"

It was about an hour before sunset and the waters in the Gulf had turned glassy smooth. The western horizon made itself a spectacle. Orange, yellow, purple with splotches of blue with a bright red ball close to dipping into the Gulf. Clouds of puffy white hung here and there as if suspended from strings.

Pots prayed, Ruddy prayed and
Commander Paul Pitts concluded his talk
with God.

Pots felt the bump. The motion of sinking
suddenly stopped. The rush of water out
side the ship's walls could be heard. The
Just Right was speeding to the surface.

34

The Key Biscayne sat poised at the spot the Just Right went down. The divers were getting ready to hit the water.

Danny had made his way to the port side of the Key Biscayne's deck. He watched out over the now calm waters of the Gulf. The Just Right hit the surface sending a spout of water a quarter mile high. The ship bobbed and shook and settle on the surface, water running off its deck. A tail fin broke the surface, larger than any whale known. It slapped the surface and a wave of water drenched the Just Right again. The red hair appeared below Danny. A woman half out of the water, nude, beautiful. She waved at Danny. He waved back. They made eye contact for a few seconds, then Danny turned and headed back to his bunk.

35

Commander Pitts stood up from his desk. He sat his empty glass down. The phone rang.

"Pitts here."

"Sir, the Just Right is on the surface. There are survivors!"

"Understood."

Pitts snuffed out his cigar, walked to the door and removed his coat and hat from the hanger. He looked up past the ceiling, past space beyond the universe.

"Thank you."

Commander Pitts closed his office door and walked down the hall. He could see out the door at the end the rain pouring down. He pulled up the collar of his raincoat as he stepped out into the weather. Back in his office, the phone rang again direct from the

Key Biscayne with the news that his friend
Captain James Philips was not among the
survivors.

Doors opened and folks made their way to
the deck of the Just Right and fresh air.
The Key Biscayne pulled up alongside the
wounded Just Right.

Rudy and Pots made it to the deck about
the same time, looking over the side at the
calm waters. They both saw the red hair
diving below the surface. Pots pulled half a
cigar from his shirt pocket and lit it with an
old bent Zippo.

"You know Rudy I believe in unicorns
too."

About the Author

Originally from Dothan, AL and now residing in Panama City, FL, Tommy retired after having a stroke a few years back. As he was recovering, he was able to pick up where he left off: Coming up with fun and inspiring stories and books for Facebook friends and anyone who likes to read.
t32408@yahoo.com

ANOTHER GREAT BOAT ADVENTURE THAT I HOPE YOU WILL ENJOY!